A story written by children
for children.

Hi Friends!

In Loving Memory of Aaron Steven McCuddin

Written by:
Allison (McCuddin) Poss, Ed.D.
Britni (McCuddin) Tondreau

Edited by:
Allison (McCuddin) Poss, Ed.D.

Illustrations by:
Kent McCuddin

Reading bedtime stories turned into making up our own stories.
This is one of our favorite made up stories.

ISBN: 978-0-578-79887-5 (Hardcover Edition)
ISBN: 978-0-578-79888-2 (Softcover Edition)

www.kentmccuddin.com

Once about a time, there was a red mouse named Tommy. Tommy just moved into a new house, and he was so excited to make friends with his new neighbors. As Tommy was unpacking

his boxes, he looked around his new street and noticed that all of his neighbors were green mice. He was nervous that they may not want to be friends with him since he was different from them.

The first few days Tommy was in his new house, he saw that the green mice gathered every day to play basketball.

Tommy would look out the window and watch them play basketball, laugh, and have fun together. This made Tommy even more nervous to introduce himself because he was not great at playing basketball.

Tommy loved making art and dancing with his old friends. He was talented at drawing, painting, and making things. He never saw green mice doing art projects though.

One day, Tommy decided he was going to be brave and ask if he could join in the basketball game. He thought that if he played basketball more, he would get better at it. So, he went outside to the basketball court to introduce himself to all of the green mice.

When he got to the court and saw all the green mice together, he got too nervous to talk to them. He turned around and went back to the house before saying anything.

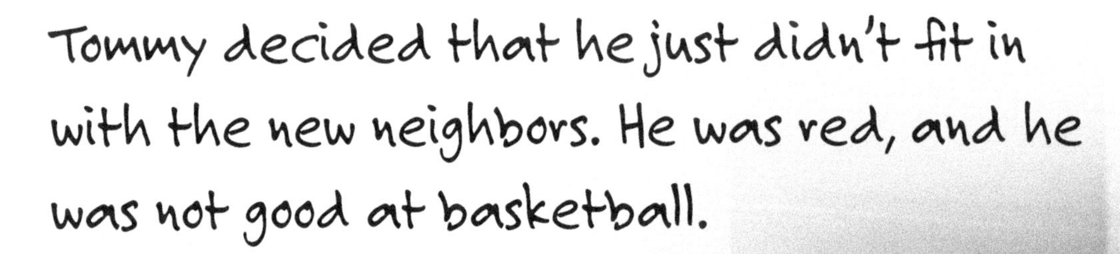

Tommy decided that he just didn't fit in with the new neighbors. He was red, and he was not good at basketball.

So, he decided to have fun on his own and make his own friends! Tommy spent the whole day drawing, painting, and cutting out life-size mice that were both red and green. He placed the friends he made all over the house.

MR
MOUSE
RADIO

With his new friends all over the house, Tommy turned on some music. He put out juice boxes and candy and started dancing with his paper friends.

The neighborhood mice were outside playing basketball and heard the music coming from Tommy's house. They looked at his house and saw a bunch of mice having fun. They thought Tommy must be really fun and wanted to go meet their new neighbor.

The green mice went to Tommy's house and knocked on the door.

"Hello! We wanted to meet you but you ran away from us when we were playing basketball. We wanted to see if we could join your party and get to know you better!"

Tommy was very excited to hear this and invited them in.

PLAID

The first thing the green neighborhood mice noticed were that the friends at Tommy's party were hand-painted. They thought that was so cool, and they asked Tommy to teach them how to make mice cut-outs.

"I didn't know you liked art! " said Tommy.

"We love trying things with new friends. We are so happy you are in our neighborhood!" the green mice said.

They spent the rest of the day partying, making even more cut-out friends, dancing, and laughing.

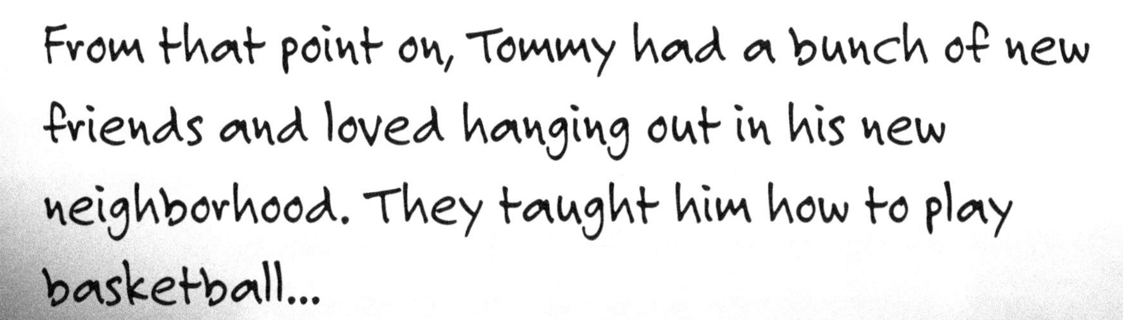

From that point on, Tommy had a bunch of new friends and loved hanging out in his new neighborhood. They taught him how to play basketball...

...and he taught them how to make cool art projects like doing chalk drawings on the court!

Making friends is so much fun.

Lightning Source UK Ltd.
Milton Keynes UK
UKHW050640221220
375282UK00012B/71